seven years from home

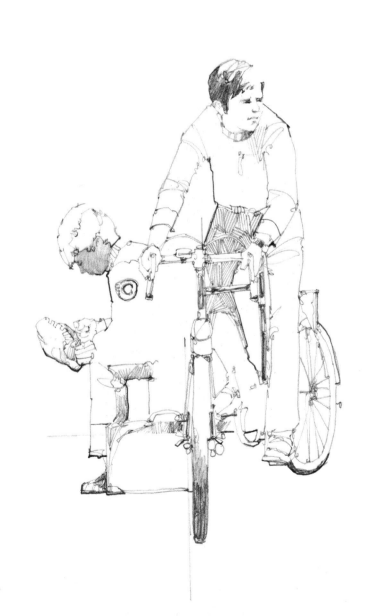

seven years from home

By Rose Blue

Illustrated by Barbara Ericksen

RAINTREE EDITIONS

Library of Congress Number: 75-42105
Printed in the United States of America

Published by 🌳 **RAINTREE EDITIONS**

A Division of Raintree Publishers Limited
Milwaukee, Wisconsin 53203

Distributed by Childrens Press
1224 West Van Buren Street
Chicago, Illinois 60607

Library of Congress Cataloging in Publication Data

Blue, Rose.
 Seven years from home.

 SUMMARY: Follows an adopted boy's emotional struggle to find his "real" parents and ultimately himself.
 (1. Adoption—Fiction) I. Ericksen, Barbara M. II. Title.
PZ7.B6248Se (Fic) 75-42105
ISBN 0-8172-0075-4
ISBN 0-8172-0076-2 lib. bdg.

The author appreciates the valuable assistance of Dr. Lillian Gross, Clinical Assistant Professor of Psychiatry at Downstate Medical Center, Diplomate of the American Board of Pediatrics, Psychiatry, and Child Psychiatry.

seven years from
home

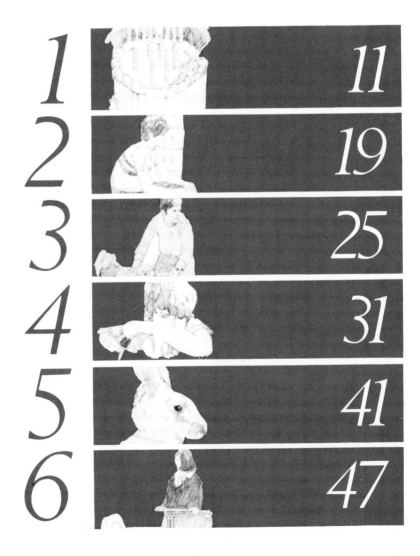

For Babs and Dini
when they grow up

seven years from home

1 Mark Cranston stepped back from the alley. The tenth frame of the second game was over, and Mark had won easily—as he nearly always did in any sport. Mark wished the rest of his life were as simple as knocking down ten pins.

"Great game, birthday boy," his friend Eric Allen said admiringly.

"Yeah, thanks. You bowled a good game, too."

Mark felt his fingers tightening inside the bowling ball. He tried to seem cool, Mark the Winner, but the hot, angry feelings flowed through him. He clenched his fingertips and tried to control the urge to fling the ball into the next alley and bust up the game of the people playing there, people he didn't even know.

"Ready, Mark?" Eric asked. "Most everybody's through."

Mark loosened his grip on the ball. His friend Eric didn't mean any harm. "Birthday boy." It was his birthday. This was his party. And he had chosen the Mixing Bowl as the place. The kids were having a good time so far. Everybody had bowled two games, and now it was time to eat. Nobody seemed to think of his birthday as any different from anybody else's. Just a birthday, just a party, just a reason to have fun.

Mark put his bowling ball back on the rack, wiped his face with his hand and passed his fingers through his longish, dark, straight hair. He put his arm on Eric's shoulder.

"Okay, buddy. Let's go eat."

The basement room of the bowling alley was set up for Mark's party. Mrs. Cranston was waiting for them there, and she smiled as everyone scrambled for seats. In a few minutes the room was filled with the aroma of pizza and the noise of kids talking and laughing above the music of the juke box. Mark kept calm, eating pizza, kidding around, and smiling. He was doing fine until the birthday cake came. The lights went out, the candles were lit, and the sounds of *Happy Birthday* replaced the juke box.

"Make a wish. Make a wish," everybody called.

Mark closed his eyes tightly and clenched his fists under the tablecloth. "I wish I knew my parents," he cried silently. "I wish I knew my parents." He inhaled deeply, then blew out all the candles with one breath.

"What did you wish for?" asked his kid brother, Peter.

"Secret," Mark said quietly.

Mark sat patiently through the rest of his party. When it was over, all the kids climbed into the cars that awaited them and rode off. Peter, Mark, and Eric jumped into the Cranston car and Mrs. Cranston drove out of the Mixing Bowl parking lot.

Mrs. Allen came out of her house when the car pulled into the Cranstons' driveway next door. She walked over, Eric's two younger sisters following close behind.

"How was the party?" she asked excitedly.

"Great, Mom," Eric said. "Real great."

"Can you believe it?" Mrs. Allen said. "Our kids are really growing up. Mark's birthday, and next month Eric's." She shook her head. "My biggest boy, and it seems like yesterday that I heard him crying in the delivery room." Mrs. Allen looked at Mark and bit her lower lip.

Mark walked quickly into the house and let the screen door slam behind him. He ran to his room and sat on the edge of the bed. Who heard him crying in that delivery room? Whose arms reached out for him? There were 11 candles on that birthday cake today. Only seven more to go. In seven more years, seven birthdays from today, he would know.

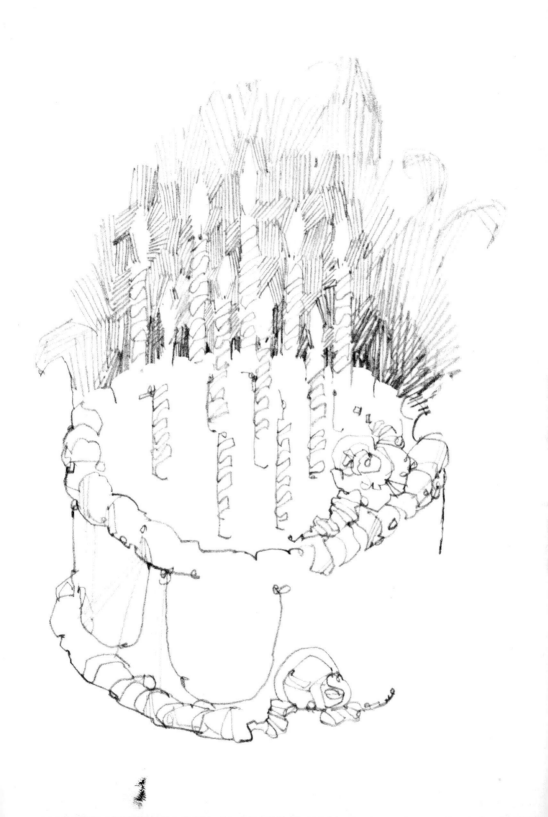

Mark slid down to the floor and sat with his chin resting on his knees. He tried to remember as far back as he could. If only he could remember back to the day he was born. Then he would remember his real mother. But his first memories went back to when he was three years old. He could remember walks with his mother and Peter when Peter was still in the baby carriage. He could remember nice things, like picnics in the park. And frightening things, like falling off his first three-wheeler bicycle and lying on the sidewalk, screaming, as his parents ran to comfort him.

His parents. Mark thought back to the Christmas Eve before his fourth birthday. He sat in the living room with his parents while Peter slept upstairs in the crib. The lighted tree glistened with colored ornaments, the angel stood perched on top, and the carefully wrapped gifts decorated the floor below.

Mark remembered his mother opening a book and reading the story of the first Christmas. Dad or Mom read to him every night, but they said this story was very special. All about Joseph and Mary and how hard it was for them to find a place for Mary to have her baby. Finally the baby was born in a manger. "And they wrapped the baby in swaddling clothes." Mark sat still until the end. He liked the story and the way Mom read it.

"Tell me about when I was born," he said.

Mom and Dad looked at each other for awhile.

"It was different when we took you home with us," Mom said at last. "You were adopted."

"What does that mean?"

"Well," Dad said, "it means we wanted a baby very much for a very long time. Then we went to find one. We saw lots and lots of tiny babies, but when we saw you we knew you were right for us. We picked you from all the other babies. You were very special and we wanted you very much."

"You mean Mom didn't have me the way Mary had her baby?"

"No," Mom said. "You grew in my heart, not in my tummy."

Mark thought of Eric's mother. Her tummy was very fat and when he asked her why, she said a baby was growing inside her. He wondered what a mommy looked like when a baby was growing in her heart.

"And Peter?" he asked. "I don't remember when Peter came."

"You were two years old," Dad said.

"Where did Peter grow?"

"In my tummy," Mom answered.

Mark tried to picture how Mom looked when he and Peter were growing inside her, but he couldn't.

"I can't wait till tomorrow to open my presents," he said.

Mark hadn't thought much more about it after that Christmas Eve. Not until he started kindergarten. Mark remembered that day very, very clearly. The kids were playing in the block corner, the painting corner, and the house corner. Mark tried out the different areas. When he got to the house corner, a little girl named Kathy handed him a hat from the dress-up carton. "Here," she said. "You be the daddy and I'll be the mommy." Two other kids said they would be the aunt and uncle.

Kathy picked up the baby doll from the wooden play crib and put the tiny bottle in its mouth. "You know," she told the other kids, "we're getting a new baby at my house. My mother is going to the hospital soon to have the baby." She looked down at the doll she was holding. "You know," she said importantly, "my mommy let me feel the baby kicking. It's growing in her tummy."

"That's not how my mommy got me," Mark said. "I grew in her heart. I was adopted."

"Oh," said a boy named Frank. "That means your folks aren't your real parents. You're not really their kid."

"What do you mean, I'm not really their kid? They're my parents and I'm their kid."

"You are not!"

"I am so!"

"Are not."

Mark pushed Frank against the wall of the house corner, noisily knocking over the screen. "I am so," he said loudly.

The kindergarten teacher came running up to them. "You're in school now," Miss Dorfman said sternly, "and this is not the way we treat each other here."

Mark remembered his mother picking him up that day. She took Eric home, too. Mark stayed very quiet but Eric talked a lot, so Mom didn't notice. Mark scrunched down in the seat listening to the sounds of the car radio and the voices of Eric and Mom as the words, "not really their kid, not really their kid," grew louder and louder in his head.

Kindergarten had been a long time ago. He'd soon found out that he hadn't really grown in his mother's heart. It made him feel even worse. How could he have been so stupid? He hadn't understood just what his parents meant when they said they had picked him out.

But even though kindergarten had been a long time ago, the meaning behind the words, "your folks aren't your real parents; you're not really their kid," stayed with him. The feelings he'd had that day grew through the years like a wall of ivy winding higher and higher around him, and made it harder and harder for him to talk about his adoption. His parents seldom discussed it, either, not knowing how much it really bothered him. Sometimes the thought that Mom and Dad weren't his real parents made him feel unreal. Then he would go out and do things to make himself feel more real, like running around the track or racing through the streets on his bike.

If only he knew who his real parents were. Then he would know who he was. Often as he walked along the street, or looked out the window of a moving car, he would spot a woman with dark black hair and hazel eyes, a woman who looked like him. And the thought that she might be his real mother would flit quickly across his mind. When he passed a pregnant woman on the street he would wonder about the woman who had carried him. How had she felt in that faraway time? How had his real mother felt before he was born, and later before she gave him away?

And why did she give him away? The terrible question had eaten away at Mark throughout the years. He kept trying to push it to the back of his mind.

Mark had never wondered out loud why he had been given away. But when he was younger, he sometimes asked who his real parents were. And each time his folks told him that they didn't know. In the last year Mark had begun to wonder more and more, perhaps because he was beginning to really grow up.

Then, a few months ago, Mark had seen a television program in which a newscaster spoke to a woman who had been adopted. She said the adoption agency didn't tell anyone who your real parents were, not even the people who adopted you. But when the woman grew up she decided to learn who her natural parents were, and she found them. Mark had made lots of phone calls the next day when nobody else was home, and he learned that at 18 some adoption agencies would tell you who your natural parents were. If they wouldn't you could hire a lawyer to get a court order and force the adoption agency to tell you your real last name. The lawyer could dig deeper and find out who your parents were. People were fighting in the courts for the right to be told everything about their natural parents at 18. Maybe by the time he was old enough, the law would be passed. But somehow, he would find out. That was for sure.

 seven years from home

2

"Mark, Mark," his mother's voice called. "Don't you hear me? I've been calling and calling. Come on down. Dad's home."

Mark sighed, stood up, and walked downstairs. The table was set for dinner; a cake with "Happy Birthday Mark" written in frosting stood in the middle.

"Hope you can manage two cakes in one day," Mom laughed. "We thought we'd have a second party, just for us."

"Sure, Mom."

"Say, son," Dad said excitedly. "I can't wait till after dinner. Come on out now and see the surprise we've got for you."

Mark followed his parents down the steps and into the garage. Leaning against the wall next to the car was a bicycle-shaped package all covered with decorated wrapping paper. It was tied with red ribbon and wore a huge card saying "Happy Birthday Mark."

"Happy Birthday," his parents said.

Mark untied the ribbon and tore the wrapping paper. He looked at the bike. It was shiny, it was new, and it was exactly like his old one.

"But that's just like the bike I have now," he said disappointedly.

"Sure. But you needed a new bike. Yours is getting shot," his father said.

"But Joe Reeves has an English racer, with ten speeds, and hand brakes, and everything."

"Joe Reeves has a much bigger house and a much richer father," his mother said.

Mark grew angry. He was Mark the Winner. That's what all the kids called him. He was best at baseball, swimming, everything. He should have a bike like Joe Reeves'.

"I bet my real parents would buy it for me," he said.

"We don't know that," his mother answered.

"I bet you'd get it for Peter if he asked."

"Peter wouldn't ask," his mother said.

"Oh sure, stick up for him. He's your real son." Mark put back the wrapping cover. "I don't want it," he said. "I don't care what you do with it."

His father sighed and put his arms around Mark. "It's your birthday, son," he said. "I guess we can cut a few corners here and there and swing the racer."

Mark stiffened in his father's arms. He was getting what he wanted. He had won. But he wasn't sure what he had won. His feelings were mixed together, like a jumbled dream you couldn't remember clearly the next morning. In one way he was ashamed of asking for the bike, a bike he knew his parents couldn't afford. Still, he felt that they had let him down by agreeing to get it. By not really coming down hard enough on him. He should have been glad about the racer, yet deep inside he couldn't push back the feeling that a real father would have stood up to his son.

Mark felt strange with his parents for the next few days. After his birthday he tried to avoid them, to spend as much time as possible away from the house. One day after school he hung around at Eric's with some of the other kids. When he got home his mother didn't even hear him come in.

She was in the living room, talking loudly, nearly yelling, something she almost never did. Mom nearly always spoke softly, and when she was angry she would stop and wait until she grew calmer before she spoke.

"I'm sorry, Martha," she said. "I won't have any part of it."

Mark passed the living room and looked inside. His mother was sitting with her friend, Mrs. Neufeld. They didn't notice him. Usually Mark would have gone

straight to his room, glad that nobody had seen him. Who wanted to hear dull grownup talk anyhow? But something in the tone of his mother's voice stopped him. He sat down on the third step, leaned against the railing, and listened.

"But why?" Mrs. Neufeld was saying. "I've been trying to get you to join the church sisterhood for years. We've done so much for the community, and you're active in many of the same causes we are."

"I know. I'm not saying that you don't do worthwhile things. And of course we go to church. But I will have nothing to do with the sisterhood."

"Again Louise, why?"

His mother didn't answer for a minute. Mark figured she was angry and was waiting to calm down before answering.

"Because of the notice I sent them when Mark was born," she blurted out.

"What notice?"

"We were so proud and happy when we got Mark. I sent a notice to the sisterhood bulletin: 'Mr. and Mrs. John Cranston announce the arrival of their son Mark.'

"When the bulletin came I looked for the announcement and didn't find it. I called Jeanette Ross, the editor of the bulletin, and asked her why. I'll never forget her answer. 'Of course we would have run the notice if it was your real child,' she said. 'But people would just get confused if we printed your announcement.' I hung up on her. Banged the phone down hard as I could and I'd do it again."

"But that was so many years ago, Louise," Mrs. Neufeld said. "And you can't judge the whole sisterhood by Jeanette Ross. Everyone knows what a birdbrain she is, anyway."

Mark got up and slipped quietly out the front door. Served him right for listening to other people's private conversations. He felt the way he did the time he watched a television program when he should have been studying, and failed a social studies test as a result. When he got his marks, he wished he hadn't watched the TV show. Now he wished he hadn't heard Mrs. Neufeld and his mother.

He got his old bike out and rode away from the block. "If it was your real child." Mark thought of all the vague childhood memories, pushed to the back of his mind. Suddenly the voices of all the visitors, doctors, and teachers blended into one loud chant: "Your adopted child. Your real child." Mark felt the hot anger. Grownups were supposed to know better. But when you were a little kid they acted like you were stupid or something, and said any old thing figuring you couldn't understand them. Mark pedaled faster and faster, riding farther and farther away until the sunshine dimmed and the twilight shadows began to fall on the quiet streets.

seven years from home

The English racer arrived about a week after Mark's birthday. His parents tried to act happy and excited about the gift, and Mark tried to feel good about getting it. But somehow it was as though he had won a prize because he had played a game in an unfair, unsportsmanlike way.

Mark rode his bike over to Joe Reeves'. Somehow he felt that if his friends got excited over the bike, he would feel better and happier about it, too. Eric and some other kids were playing pool in the large basement playroom. They all came running out to see Mark's bike.

"That's a great looking bike," Joe said. "It's a lot like mine, too."

"Yeah," Eric said, running his fingers over the handlebars. "I'd never get a bike like that. Mark's lucky. He got that English racer and his folks aren't even really," Eric paused a second and his hands tightened on the bars, "really rich."

Mark looked away. He knew Eric had nearly said, "aren't really his parents." He knew that Eric hadn't meant to hurt him. That he just got jealous for a second because he couldn't have a racer. But deep down in Eric's mind it was there. That Mark's folks weren't his own. This wasn't the first time. Kids had slipped, or nearly slipped, before. Would things like this never stop happening? And was that why he wanted to be Mark the Winner? To have more and be better than anyone else? Because they all had something of their own he never had? Their real parents?

Joe put his arm around Mark's shoulder and tried to sound light and cheerful. "Hey, come on in and join the game. You play pool better than anybody here."

That night at dinner Mark was quiet. He couldn't drive the afternoon from his mind. But when he looked up he saw that something else was wrong. Peter kept rolling his food around on his plate, not saying much. "You know," Peter said after awhile, "my birthday is in May. That's not even two months from now."

"That's right," Mom said. "We'll be planning another birthday soon."

"Time flies," Dad said. "Peter's nearly nine years old."

"Richard's brother has his own horse," Peter said suddenly.

"He does?" Mom asked.

"He rides in horse shows. He's 15 and he owns a horse. His parents bought it for him. They keep the horse at Championship Farms. Richard's brother Steven goes to the farm and rides him. and works him out."

"That's an interesting hobby," Dad said.

"Sure is. And you know what? Richard goes along with Steven and helps him take care of the horse. He curries and grooms him and everything. I was there yesterday and Richard's dad drove us out. I helped take care of the horse."

"It must have been fun," Mom said.

"Yeah." Peter rolled his food around some more. "That's what I want for my birthday," he blurted out. "A horse. Then I could keep it at the farm and care for it and train it. I'm real good with animals."

His parents looked at each other.

"Yes. You're great with animals," Dad said, "but I'm afraid that's impossible. First of all, you're much too young. Richard's brother is 15. And even if you were old enough, we could never afford it now. It would be terribly expensive."

"You got what Mark wanted," Peter said. He knocked his plate across the table. "Mark gets everything," he shouted. He jumped up, ran to his room and banged the door. Mom and Dad went after

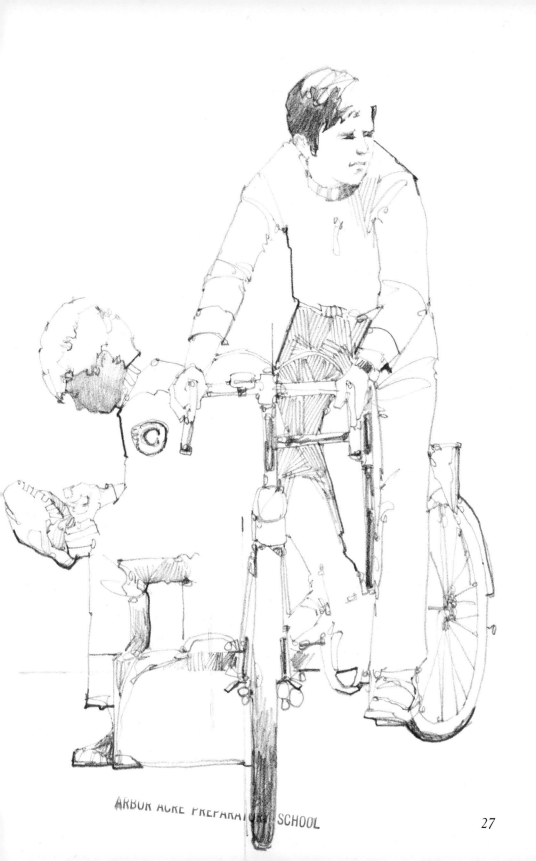

ARBOR ACRE PREPARATORY SCHOOL

him, with Mark close behind.

Dad put his hand on Mark's wrist. "Maybe you'd better let your mother and me talk to him first." Mark went to his room and sat on his bed as the voices came from Peter's room, soft and loud tones mingling like a stereo record.

"He always gets what he asks for, even if it does cost a lot of money," Peter yelled.

"But he is older," Mom said.

"Yeah," Peter said bitterly. "And taller and handsomer and better at sports. Nobody cares about me."

"Of course we do," Dad was saying. "We all care very much."

"No you don't," Peter said. "You give everything to him because he's adopted."

"Now, Peter," Mom started to say, but the loudness of Peter's crying overpowered the soft sound of her voice.

"Maybe we'd better leave the boy alone now, Louise, and talk another time when things are calmer."

Mark heard his parents walk out of Peter's room. He heard Peter's door closing softly, then his parents' door. He left his room. His parents were talking together in low, quiet tones.

Mark knocked on Peter's door, knocked again, and walked in. Peter lay on his bed, sobbing loudly into his pillow. Mark didn't know why he had come, why he felt like he had done something very wrong, or what to do now that he was here. He just knew that Peter wasn't such a bad little kid and that he ought to do something to quiet him down. He leaned against the wall, then walked toward Peter's bed.

"Hey, kid," he said softly. "Want to talk?"

"Go away," Peter said, turning his head toward the wall.

Mark walked nearer to Peter.

"Go away," Peter said between sobs. "Just go away and leave me alone. Nobody cares about me. They picked you." Mark walked toward the door and left the room as his brother's sobs grew stronger. "They had to take me," Peter wept, chokingly. "They had to take me."

Mark was due to go to Scouts after school the next afternoon. But Mr. Borgen, the scoutmaster, was sick and the session was canceled. Mark was worried about Peter so he went straight home after school instead of trying to find his friends. He opened the front door, put his books on the table and headed toward the sound of voices coming from the living room.

"You have to try to understand, Peter," Dad was saying. "Try not to feel . . ." Dad looked up and saw Mark standing in the doorway. "Hi," he said. "What are you doing home?"

Mark looked around at everyone. Mom and Dad were sitting on the sofa, with Peter between them. Peter looked very sad and Mom and Dad looked serious and troubled.

"Mr. Borgen got sick so we had no Scouts. How come you're home?"

"I had a meeting that ended early," his father said.

"What's going on here, anyway?" Mark asked.

"Nothing," Mom said, trying to sound calm. "Nothing at all."

Mark walked partway into the room. The place got so quiet you would have thought everyone had vanished into thin air. He turned and walked away quickly. He picked up his books, ran upstairs and slammed his door.

Mark knew that if one of their children was very troubled, Mr. and Mrs. Cranston would talk privately to him. He knew that a person was entitled to privacy, but Peter had turned away from him when he tried to help. And now the folks had stopped talking to Peter the minute they saw Mark's face, like he was some kind of a stranger.

Why was it that his parents could talk to Peter about his adoption but found it so difficult to discuss it with him? In the past he'd often hoped they'd talk more freely about it, since he found it so hard to bring up his worries himself. Now he decided he did not want their help. He had tried to come too close and they had all locked him out. He went back to avoiding the family and hanging around outside as much as possible.

seven miles from home

March in the suburbs was warm that year. The sun shone bright, the trees began to bud, and the kids began playing baseball early. The elementary school kids practiced baseball in a field in Elton Park and Mark spent a good deal of his time there. He belonged to a town league for boys.

One Saturday morning Peter came down from his room. "I can't find my glove," he said. "And I'm going to play baseball today."

Mark looked up from his breakfast. "Oh," he said casually. "I took it."

"Why'd you take my glove?" Peter asked indignantly. "You have your own."

"I looked at mine before spring practice. The leather on the palm was ripped. Makes it harder to catch the ball. So I took yours."

"You had no right to take Peter's glove," Mrs. Cranston said.

Mark shrugged. "I liked it better than mine and I needed a glove."

"That's no excuse for borrowing what doesn't belong to you without even asking," Mrs. Cranston said.

"I figured to keep it," Mark said coolly, "till you get a new one for me. Peter's is newer than mine."

"We haven't even talked about a new glove," Mr. Cranston said angrily. "But we sure will talk about taking what isn't yours. That glove belongs to Peter."

"I should have a new glove," Mark said, his voice beginning to lose its cool. "Your real son does. I should have what I need. My real parents would give it to me. They're rich. I know it."

"That's enough of that," Mrs. Cranston said. "We're not rich. I do know that much. And we talk over what we need and how to spend our money."

"Well, I should have money in my own pocket to spend on what I want."

"I'm afraid we don't have a money tree in the backyard," Mr. Cranston said sarcastically. "If you felt you needed a new glove you should have said so. Then we could have discussed it. But what is most serious is that you took your brother's glove. That glove belongs to Peter. Now go and get it and give it back to him. And I mean now!"

Mark might have felt better about his dad laying down the law like a real father if Dad hadn't taken Peter's side against him. But Mark had been feeling so left out of everything lately, especially since Mom and Dad kept having private talks with Peter. Maybe he took Peter's glove to get back at Peter and his folks for acting like he wasn't part of the family. Maybe he took the glove because he wanted more than Peter had. Because Peter seemed to have a family, and right now Mark didn't. He got mad and started to answer, but something in his father's face stopped him. He got up sullenly, walked upstairs slowly, and came back with the glove. "Here," he said, throwing the glove on the floor near Peter's feet. "Take your old glove. You couldn't catch a mosquito if you wore the best glove in town."

Mark kept avoiding his family. He was an outsider in that house anyway. One Saturday he got up early, went jogging, and found Eric and some of the other kids at the handball court in back of Elton Park. He played ball awhile, then hung around at Eric's house. He would have stayed at Eric's longer but the Allens were going out. He cut through the Allens' side lawn and climbed over the fence into his own yard, as he often did. He heard voices coming from the back and walked toward the patio.

Grandma was there. He began to run toward her. Grandma lived in the city and had refused to move from her apartment although Grandpa had died six years ago. She said it was her home and she wouldn't

live with her children. They visited her and she came out to visit. But her apartment was a distance away and Mark didn't see as much of her as he would have liked. Grandma was okay. She really seemed like his grandma, and he never felt adopted when he was with her.

"I swear I don't know what to do," Mom was saying. Her voice was loud and shaky.

Mark knew that he shouldn't be eavesdropping. He had regretted listening to his mother and Mrs. Neufeld that day. It was wrong to listen to people's private conversations, and besides, you didn't always like what you heard. Yet lately Mark felt a very strong sense of being on the outside looking in. It was as though the family only talked about important things when they thought he wasn't around. He sat under the tree behind the patio and listened.

"The more I do for Mark the more he wants. Then Peter starts demanding more. Even wild, ridiculous things. There are a few very wealthy families in this area, but we're not among them. After all, John is an engineer and with the economy the way it is, business is shaky. I do substitute teaching when I can, but expenses are high and we can afford only so much."

"Then just explain it to the kids," Grandma said. "They're old enough to understand."

"It's not that easy. All I ever wanted was to have a real family and be a mother to both my sons. But Peter says we do more for Mark because he's adopted, and Mark keeps saying we care more for Peter because Peter's our real child."

"Nonsense," Grandma said. "They're both yours. My grandsons are my grandsons and that's that!"

Mark believed Grandma really felt that way. But often when the family sat together at dinner, Mark would look at them and feel as though he had been invited to eat at somebody else's house. His mother, his grandmother, and Peter all had blond hair, blue eyes, and fair skin. His father had sandy hair and blue eyes, and his skin was very fair, too. Mark looked nothing like any of them, with his dark hair and olive complexion.

Then there was the time at the doctor's office. Mark had kept sneezing and getting rashes and nobody could figure out why. Dr. Thompson said Mark was probably allergic to certain things and sent him to a special doctor.

"We'll take tests," the new doctor had said. "But first I want a family history. Does anyone else in your family suffer from allergies?"

Mrs. Cranston squirmed in her chair. Dr. Lesser didn't know that Mark was adopted.

"Mark is our adopted son," she had said.

"I see. Well, the tests will tell us what the problem is."

Dr. Lesser cured Mark's rashes and sneezes, but his question made Mark feel worse than the allergies had. He might never be able to tell any doctor what illnesses anyone in his family had. What if there was something wrong with his real folks? Something he could pass on to his own kids someday? Joe Reeves' father had diabetes, and Joe was always being tested for it. What if there was something like that in Mark's real family? He must find his real parents so he would know.

"Mark is becoming just impossible," his mother was saying now. "I don't know how to handle him."

"You're making too much of it, Louise."

"No. We were so happy when we got Mark. We had such high hopes for him. He was just a perfect little baby. We had wanted a baby for so long, and the doctor thought we might never be able to have one of our own."

Mark thought of all the times his parents told him that they had picked him because he was special. Now his mom was talking like she had made a mistake. Like he had been picked because they wanted a special kind of son, and he wasn't turning out right. He was a disappointment.

A picture of his mom at the supermarket came to his mind. Mark often went with her. Mom was always squeezing the melons, trying to pick out the best ones. But sometimes when she opened a melon for dinner it would be too dry or over-ripe. "I can't understand it," she would say. "I picked so carefully."

Mark climbed quietly over Eric's fence, then back down again to his own yard, making as much noise as he could. He ran toward the patio.

"Grandma," he called loudly. "I'm glad you're here."

He ran to his grandma. She held his face in her hands. "My big, handsome grandson," she said. She pulled him close to her the way she always did. He hugged her tight and let his cheek rest against hers like he was still little. Being nearer to Grandma made him feel more like a kid somebody loved and less like a melon in the market.

Grandma stayed all day and Mark felt better than he had in a long time. He felt warmer and calmer and a little more like he belonged someplace. After dinner Mom and Dad invited Grandma to spend the rest of the weekend with them.

"Next time," Grandma said. "I don't have my night clothes and some other things I need here. When you get older you need your own things with you."

"Okay, Mom," Dad said. "Next time come ready to spend more time with us. I'll drive you home later."

"Grandma," Mark said on an impulse, "can I come home with you and sleep over?"

"Grandma doesn't have room," Dad said. "And it would be a lot of trouble."

"What kind of trouble?" Grandma said. "Didn't I ever have children in my house? It will be fun. If Mark doesn't mind the living room couch."

"I don't mind, Grandma."

"We can go to the outdoor art show tomorrow," Grandma said. "Next time Peter can stay with me."

"All right," Dad said. "Then we'll pick up Mark late tomorrow afternoon."

"Good," Grandma said. "Then it's settled."

Mark looked out the window during the long drive to Grandma's, spotting women who looked like him. Often when he rode in a car he would imagine he was on his way home, to his real home, though he had no idea of where that was. When he got to Grandma's he had a feeling of adventure, but calm, comfortable adventure, a feeling of coming home.

Grandma made him some cocoa and then fixed up the couch. The afghan that she had crocheted was warm and cozy and Mark snuggled against it and fell

into a sound sleep. When he awoke he rubbed his eyes and sat up irritably. That dream again. He'd had that same dream ever since kindergarten, and lately it had been coming more frequently.

The dream was not really clear. He was lost and he kept trying to get back home. He wasn't sure which home he was dreaming about, the Cranston house or the home of his real parents. But in the dream he kept wandering around a maze of strange streets and getting more and more lost. When he was little the dream would awaken him suddenly and he would be very frightened for awhile. He would think that someday when he got big he would want to go to his real home and he wouldn't know the way. Now that he was older the dream no longer frightened him so, but it was annoying and disturbing.

He tried to go back to sleep but he was wide awake. Grandma's apartment was silent. Grandma was still asleep and he didn't want to walk around and wake her. He got up and sat on a chair near the living room window. The sun was beginning to rise. Mark looked down at the street below. He liked the view. It was very different from the suburban lawns. The houses were high and close together. There was life and movement on the street even though it was early Sunday morning. A few people seemed to be coming home from a night out, dressed in evening clothes. Other people seemed to be leaving their houses on their way to work. There were all kinds of jobs people might be going to on a city Sunday. Maybe to work in bakeries, or hospitals, or restaurants, or any of dozens of places. Mark watched the people and the sunrise, and thought of the dream that had awakened him.

How much longer would he have to dream of home? Of looking for a place he could not find? Mark had sometimes thumbed through the books about animals that Peter was always borrowing from the library. So many other living things found their way to places by instinct. Swallows, salmon at spawning time, and elephants when it was time to die. If only he could find

his real home the same way.

Mark looked at the sun. It lit up the street now. Morning had come and people were walking in greater numbers, dressed as though for church. Mark heard Grandma moving around the kitchen. He left the living room.

"Hi, Grandma," he said. "Can I help?"

She ran her hand through his hair and kissed his cheek. "No thanks, honey. I'll make breakfast. You just get ready and let me spoil my grandson."

The visit to Grandma's was like running away for a little while. But when it ended, nothing had changed. Mark kept staying away from his family's house as much as he could and saying as little as he could to his parents and Peter.

seven years from home

One day when he came home from Eric's, Mark found his parents and Peter in the backyard. Peter was holding something in his arms.

"What's going on?" Mark asked.

"Easter is early this year," Dad said. "And so are the animal problems."

"What?"

"I found a baby rabbit in the grass near Elton Park," Peter said. "I guess somebody bought it for Easter and just threw it away when it got to be too much trouble. And it isn't even Easter yet."

"That's terrible."

"You bet. I'm going to build a hutch and keep it out back and take care of it."

"Great. Here. Let's see."

Peter held out the rabbit. Mark came closer, reached his hand over to pet the animal, and began sneezing violently.

"I forgot that I'm allergic to fur," he said between sneezes. He waved. "See you," he said, and ran into the house.

Mark sat on his bed after the sneezing finally stopped. He picked up his math book and was starting to do his homework when the sneezing began again. He looked up and saw Peter standing over him.

"Why didn't they get rid of you when I came?" Peter yelled.

"What?" Mark looked puzzled.

"Our folks," Peter burst out chokingly. "They picked you when they didn't have a baby. Then I was born. Why couldn't they just give you back?"

Mark started to get angry, but Peter looked so little and miserable.

"What's the matter?" he said evenly. "Just tell me what happened."

"I can't keep the rabbit," Peter sobbed, "because you're allergic."

"But the rabbit's outside."

"I know. But I'll bring the hairs into the house on my clothes, and you'll have to pass the rabbit every time you walk through the yard."

It was true. Mark had sneezed walking from the yard and again when Peter came in.

"I'm sorry, kid," he said.

"You get everything you need for sports. I don't get anything. I love animals. Remember that year you went to the allergy doctor? Mom and Dad were going to give me a dog that summer. I even had a name picked out. And then they said no! I couldn't even have a dog because of you."

Mark got up, left the house, and rode away on his bike without saying a word to anyone. When he got back he walked straight to Peter's room and opened the door without knocking. Peter turned his face to the wall.

"I just came from Joe Reeves'," Mark said. "And it's all set. You can keep the rabbit there."

Peter sat up. "What are you talking about?"

"They've got loads of space. They're rich. We'll all build the hutch and you can keep the rabbit there. They'll see that it has everything it needs. But it will be your rabbit and you can care for him whenever you want to go. It's just a few minutes away. The Reeves said you can keep some clothes there to wear when you touch the rabbit. Then you can shower and change. They've got a shower right in their yard near the pool just like at the beach. Then you can come home and no sneezes. Okay?"

Peter swallowed and blinked. "Thanks," he said.

"Sure."

Peter swallowed again. "I didn't mean it. What I said before."

"I know."

"If our folks gave you back they could give me back too, if I made them mad or anything. You can't just throw away a kid like a bunny or a baby chick at Easter time." Peter looked down at the floor.

"Come on," Mark said quietly. "Get your bike and we'll go over to Joe's and start building the hutch."

That night Mark sat up suddenly, wide awake in the dark room. He knew he couldn't fall back to sleep again, and he hoped that sunrise was near so that he wouldn't have to wait too long to start the day. He switched on his night table lamp and looked at the face of his clock radio. It was only 5 a.m. Then it struck Mark that it was Saturday morning. There was no school today. He would have to stay in his room even longer than usual. The family would be sleeping late and so would all his friends.

He pounded his pillow. That same dream. Why did it keep coming back? And why did it wake him and keep him awake in the quiet nights when the dawn was so very far away? He kept thinking of that dream, of being lost in strange streets.

But why tonight? Why had the dream come tonight?

"Why didn't they get rid of you when I came?" Peter's words came back to Mark. Those words must have stuck in his mind and stayed there, even while he slept.

"I didn't mean it," Peter had said later. And Mark believed him. But there was something in those words that the kid did mean. A feeling that if it weren't for Mark, Peter would get more things that he wanted. That because of Mark he couldn't even have the dog that he longed for so badly.

Mark wasn't sure just why he had gone to so much trouble to help Peter keep his rabbit. His feelings about Peter were jumbled and confused. Mark was so tall that he looked older than 11, and Peter, who was not even 9 yet, often seemed little and babyish. Lately Mark had felt sorry for Peter once in awhile, and thought he should help and protect him more.

It was true that it sometimes seemed that Mark was

given more things than Peter. But didn't he deserve them? Wasn't he older, and bigger, and stronger? And what was he being given that Peter didn't have? Things. Just things you could pay for with money and buy in a store. Sometimes, deep down, Mark wished his parents would give him fewer of the things he asked for, would say no, would give him more of the caring things you didn't have to pay for.

Peter had something you couldn't buy with money. Peter had his real parents. He knew who they were. And they had never left him. Mark touched his hand to his hair and felt himself pulling at the straight, dark strands. His hair was a constant reminder that he wasn't born to the couple he called his mother and father. He felt sure that if he could find his real parents, they would make everything all right. They must have been looking for him. They must have had to give him away because they were too young or poor to keep him, and then afterwards tried hard to find him. They must be kind people, loving and understanding. He knew that by now they were wise, and strong, and rich.

Yet if his real parents were all he daydreamed they were, couldn't they have found some way to keep him? Even if things were rough for them? Why did they give him up? Who left him in that hospital nursery, and why?

Mark heard the shower running and saw that daybreak was starting to light his room at last. He waited for awhile, then got out of bed and washed. He went downstairs and found his mother in the kitchen.

"You're up early, Mark," she said. "Didn't you sleep?"

"I got up early. How come you're up?"

"Dad went to the office this morning. There's a new rush job, and with business the way it is, Dad can't afford to turn down any work. Mr. Dawson picked him up and drove him. I needed the car. I'm driving Peter to a birthday party this afternoon. And I have to go to the market after breakfast."

"Want me to help?"

Mom nodded. "I could use some help. I taught Thursday and Friday and couldn't get the shopping done. I thought Dad would come with me today."

"Okay. No sweat."

sev *s from home*

Mark carried a large bag of groceries in each arm. You had to leave the cart inside the store and carry the bags to the car yourself. There were boys helping, but Saturday morning was so busy that it was easier to carry your own groceries.

Mark shifted the bags and walked through the parking lot with his mother. The car was three aisles down. Suddenly he felt a hand brushing against his arm and heard a woman's voice saying, "Excuse me." He looked up and saw her clearly. She was tall, with straight dark hair and hazel eyes. She was old enough to be his mother, and she looked just like him. She started to walk past him, carrying her bag to her car, and Mark whirled around, bumping into her. Her bag fell to the ground, along with both of Mark's packages. The woman's bag didn't break, but one of Mark's did, and the groceries scattered around the row of the parking lot.

Mark picked up the woman's bag first and stood staring at her. "I'm sorry," he said.

"That's okay. It was partly my fault." The woman held out her hands for the bag, but Mark kept standing there, staring.

"Give the lady the bag, Mark," his mother said impatiently.

"Oh, sure." He handed the bag to the woman and watched her get into a green compact with a black vinyl top and drive away.

"Now can we try to salvage the groceries?" Mom asked. "The fruit is squashed and I don't know what

else is ruined. And at these prices."

"I'm sorry, Mom."

She rested her package on the fender of a car and placed Mark's other package nearby. They searched for the scattered groceries.

"Accidents happen, Mark," Mom said evenly. "Even to someone as fast on his feet as you are." Mark and his mother bent to find the rest of the groceries. Her eyes met his. "But I saw you staring at that woman. That's why you dropped the groceries. You couldn't take your eyes off her because she looked like you." Her voice began to rise. "All these years. All the things we did for you and you're still staring, still searching. Don't you appreciate anything?"

Mark looked down. "Of course, Mom. But I've told you someday I would have to find my real parents."

Mom waited a minute to speak, the way she did when she tried to keep calm. But when she spoke her voice rose again, until she was shouting in the crowded parking lot.

"I hope that you do find them," she yelled. "I hope that they're bums." She bent down to the ground and picked up a nearly-squashed apple. "I hope you find them in the gutter."

Mom drove home in silence. She pulled into the driveway and Mark helped carry the groceries in. He put the bags on the kitchen counter and started for the side door. Mom put her arm on his shoulder. He didn't turn.

"Please, Mark," she said. "Please wait." She hugged him tightly. He could feel her tears running down his neck. "I'm so sorry. I didn't mean what I said. I've just been so terribly upset. Can you forgive me?"

Mark thought of all the times lately that his mother, always in control, had lost her cool.

"Sure, Mom," he said quietly. He still couldn't turn. She was upset. It was true. And he knew he was a part of it. But he still couldn't face her. They'd all waited too long to discuss his worries, and now it was too hard to begin. "Sure," he said. He slipped out of her grip, walked through the side door, and leaped the fence to Eric's house.

Nobody answered Eric's doorbell. Mark pressed the bell again. He began feeling stupid, standing there pressing a doorbell that nobody answered. He leaped back over the fence, got his bike and rode to the school grounds. Somehow he felt that he had to keep moving. He parked the bike and ran around the track. The midafternoon sun grew stronger and a hungry feeling was beginning to grow in Mark's stomach. Still he did not feel ready to go home. He got back on his bike and headed for Joe Reeves' house.

He stood pushing and pushing the bell until the chimes rang in his ears. There was nobody home at Joe's either. Mark thought of riding back home but then decided to wait awhile. Maybe the Reeves had just gone to the store or something. Maybe they'd be home soon. He walked his bike around back and way past the rabbit hutch. He sat in a cool spot under a tree shaded by pale, new leaves. A tired feeling was beginning to hit him. Riding his bike and running the track didn't usually tire him. Maybe it was because he had slept so little last night. He leaned back against the tree trunk and closed his eyes.

When he opened them the sun was down and the yard was blanketed in shadows. He rubbed his eyes. It must be very late—past dinner time. He walked his bike out front. There were no lights on in the Reeves' house. They must still be gone. He got back on his bike and rode home through the twilight-dimmed streets.

When he got near his house, he saw that his parents and Peter were standing out front. The voices of Mom and Dad came at him like two television sets playing loudly and turned to different channels.

"Where have you been?"

"Do you know what time it is?"

"Why didn't you call?"

"We've been frantic."

"Are you all right?"

"Thank heavens you're home."

When the voices died down, Mark explained what had happened. "I couldn't help it. I just fell asleep," he finished.

"Okay," Dad said. "But you should have come home before you went to Joe's."

"You had us worried sick," Mom said. "I called your dad to come home from the office. I called all over and drove around everyplace."

Their voices were angry now. Grownups. First they were so happy you were home safe, and then they yelled at you for worrying them. It was like last year when Eric got a new bike. He wasn't careful and he hit a tree and fell to the sidewalk. His parents came running to see if he was hurt, and when they saw he was okay they yelled at him for damaging his bike. Mark sighed.

"I'm sorry. But I'm starving and thirsty. Got anything to eat?"

Mark sat down at the dinner table and began gulping down his food.

"Don't eat so quickly," Mom said. "It's bad for you on an empty stomach." She looked at Peter. "You've hardly touched a bite. Too much birthday cake at Abby's party?"

"I didn't get any cake," Peter exploded. "I missed the whole thing. I got there late because you were so busy stopping off everywhere looking for Mark. And then I had to wait and wait when the party was over. All the kids got picked up but me. I don't count around here." He turned to Mark. "It's all your fault."

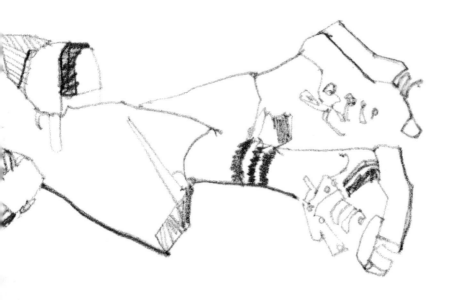

"I'm sorry about your party, kid," Mark said. He stood up and took his glass to the refrigerator to get some more milk. He was still dying of thirst.

He filled his glass and carried it back to the table. Suddenly he lost his balance and the milk spilled all over the floor. He hung onto the glass, tried not to fall, and looked down at the sticky kitchen floor. Peter's foot was stuck out, but he was looking straight ahead, all innocence. That rotten little kid had tripped him. And on purpose. All at once Mark got mad. Mad at his mom, mad at his dad, mad at the Allens and the Reeves for not being home today, but most of all right now, right at this minute, mad at Peter. He put down the glass, pulled Peter from his chair and slapped him hard across the face.

Peter stepped on his brother's foot, stamping down as hard as he could, and Mark winced in pain. Mark stepped back and kicked Peter squarely in the shins. In a minute the boys were sliding all over the wet kitchen floor.

Dad stepped in and pulled the boys apart, holding them firmly at arms' length.

"I'm ashamed of you, Mark," Dad said. "Fighting with your younger brother."

"Sure, blame me. He started it. That sweet little kid stuck his foot out and tripped me."

"He started it," Peter said. "It's all his fault."

"I did not," Mark said. "He started it."

"All right," Dad said. "That's enough. Now we're all going into the living room for a family talk." He let go of his sons. "Into the living room. Both of you."

Mom and Dad sat together on the couch. Peter walked slowly into the living room and stood in the middle of the rug as Mark lingered at the door.

"Now sit down, both of you," Dad said firmly. "Right now."

Peter walked slowly to a chair. Mark stood in the doorway for a split second longer, looked at Dad, then walked in and sat down.

"Now, boys," Dad said, "your mother and I have had enough of your behavior lately. You kids have been getting impossible. And I mean both of you."

54

"It's his fault," Peter said.

"You blame me for everything," Mark said. "Like tonight. He started it and you blamed me because he's your real son."

"Now look, Mark," Mom said angrily. She paused for a moment, and when she spoke again her voice was calmer. "I've had it with this business about my real son. I have two sons and I love them both. The first time I held you in my arms you were my son. I was thrilled. Just as I was when I first held Peter. I cared for you when you were a baby. I raised you and I'm your mother. That's why I get so upset when you talk this way." Her voice grew softer. "How do you think any woman would feel if her son kept telling her she wasn't his mother?"

Mark swallowed hard and looked down at the rug as his mother's words sank in. He should have known how she was feeling. All his life, people had kept reminding him that he wasn't her real son. And now he kept telling her that she wasn't his real mother. He was doing to her what others had done to him. His mom didn't deserve it, and he was old enough to know that he wasn't being fair.

"I couldn't possibly add anything to what your mother said about our feelings." Dad's voice grew tender. He paused, turned toward Mark and spoke in a more serious tone. "Now, Mark, I can understand your curiosity about your natural parents. And when you're of age, if you still want to, you can try to learn all you can about them and find them if possible. But that won't change the fact that we're your parents. That's how we see it. I can only repeat that you're our sons and we do love you both." His voice grew firmer. "So we try to raise you the right way. And that means you follow the rules in this house. And one of those rules is about fighting. Right?"

Mark and Peter nodded.

"Okay. Now, you both have broken that rule. And done quite a job of it, too. And I don't want to hear one word about whose fault it was. From where I sit you're both to blame and that's it." He looked at his wife. "Louise, do you agree that they should be punished?"

Mom nodded. "I agree with you, John."

"Okay. Now, how long should their punishment last?"

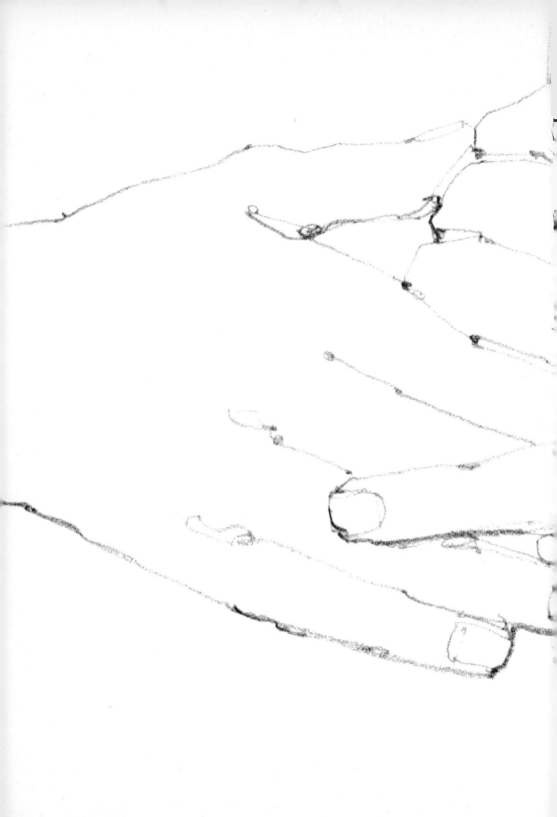

"Well," Mom said, "Easter Sunday's a week from tomorrow. I think that if the boys toe the line we should end their punishment next Saturday night and let them enjoy their holiday."

"Good idea. Then it's one week. I say they're both benched for a solid week. Really benched. They come home straight from school and stay home. No playing with friends. And no TV either. Agreed, Louise?"

Mark looked at his mother. He thought she was getting ready to say that the ban on TV was too harsh. But he knew that his parents would never argue about anything like that in front of their children.

"Agreed, John," Mom said.

"Then it's settled. And starting right now," Dad said. He stood up and pointed to the hallway. "Now, upstairs, both of you. Scoot."

Mark and Peter got up and left the living room quietly. They walked upstairs together. Peter stopped at the top of the steps and turned to Mark. "Boy, they really laid it on us. And Dad sure was tough."

"He sure was!" Mark said. His voice was proud.

Peter walked toward his room and looked at his brother. "Friends?" he asked quietly.

Mark squeezed Peter's shoulder gently. "Friends, kid," he said.

Mark went into his room, shut the door, and turned on the light. He looked at the clock radio. It was 9 o'clock. *Farrigan's Files,* his favorite detective show, was just about starting. He sat on the edge of his bed. If he put the TV set on real low, and sat very close, nobody would hear it. For just one single split second he let his hand lightly touch the switch. Then he leaned back in bed, reached over to the night table for his social studies book, and turned to the assignment for Monday.

Rose Blue is a writer and Headstart teacher who lives in Brooklyn, New York. She began her writing career with short stories and song lyrics, but soon moved into children's literature. Ms. Blue has a B.A. degree from Brooklyn College and has done graduate work at the Bank Street College. She has been contributing editor and has contributed to *Teacher* magazine. *Seven Years From Home* is Ms. Blue's 11th book.